CONTENTS

Draw your own pictures

JAMIE'S JOY

Jamie and Claire are happy dogs –
Their little pup is wearing clogs.

He walks a bit on bended knees,
Looking for the front-door keys.

He stops and sniffs his tiny bowl,
And eats a scrap of chicken roll.

What fun they have this summer's day –
Eating, drinking, having play!

Draw your own pictures

Colour in yourself

DAN

Their little pup has got a name.
He is a boy, he's not a dame.

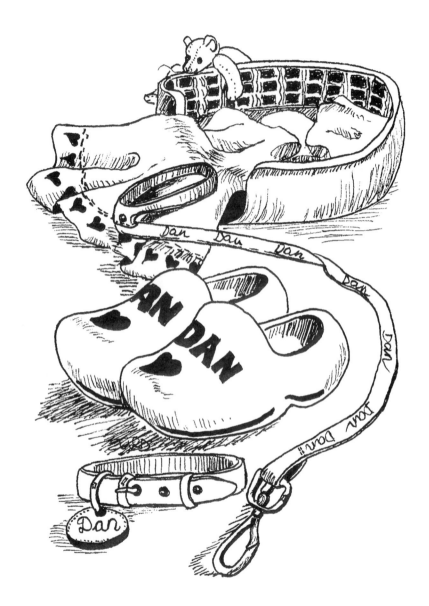

His name is written on his clogs,
So he can talk to other dogs.

Claire slips the collar round his neck.
Jamie barks, keeps him in check.

Biff arrives, brings him a ball.
"Come here, Dan," we hear Claire call.

Yes, Dan's his name, their little son,
Eating, drinking, having fun.

Draw your own pictures

Draw your own pictures

Colour in yourself

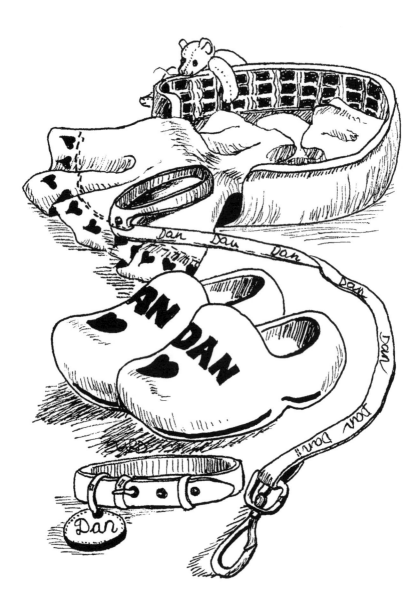

DAN IN TROUBLE

Dan has other toys at home.
He plays with them, he does not roam.

He kicks the ball with tiny feet.
The clogs fly off, oh what a treat!

He dances, sings and has a ball,
But dearie me, the hall!

Jamie shouts, "Look at that!"
And poor Claire eats her hat.

What a palaver, what a din!
All the food goes in the bin.

Draw your own pictures

Draw your own pictures

Colour in yourself

SUMMER SOLSTICE

Jamie barks, "Let's light a fire
And dress in different attire."

The summer solstice is tonight –
Dan can stay up, it's only right.

Claire just nodded, pleased with Dan.
He really was her only son.

Now Jealous Joe joined in the scene;
The rocket whooshed, quite keen.

"Oh, cool!" barked Scott, just looking on.
The eve was long – an aeon! *

*Note: 'aeon' is pronounced 'eon'. It means in
astronomy and geology a unit of time equal to 1,000
million years.

Draw your own pictures

Draw your own pictures

Colour in yourself

BEDTIME

Jamie and Dan
Are happy dogs.

The sky is cool –
They sleep like logs.

Snoring, dozing,
Dreaming long,

Claire cocks an ear
To the birdsong.

Draw your own pictures

Draw your own pictures

Colour in yourself

NEXT DAY

Claire meekly
Is shopping weekly!

Draw your own pictures

THAT SAME WEEK

Roaming round his corner plot,
Dan didn't like to feel so hot!

His mum brought out a swimming pool –
"Now just be good, don't be a fool!"

Dan dipped his paws in the shallow bit –
"Where's my trunks, my swimming kit?"

Dan paddled in the water cool –
"Now just keep safe, that is a rule."

A bee flew down and stung his nose;
Jamie splashed him with the garden hose.

Dan just bit the rubber through
And Claire stood there, feeling a little blue.

As water drained through and soaked the flowers
Jamie chilled, feeling the showers.

So the day came to an end
With Dan deciding he was on the mend.

Draw your own pictures

Draw your own pictures

Colour in yourself

IN TROUBLE AGAIN

Dan greets the postie the next day,
But a grey mouse gets in the way.

Dan barks, "Dad, look at this young mouse –
It's not allowed in our own house."

Jamie dashed to the garden gate,
Where the mouse feared for his own fate.

Dan just sniffed at the air with glee –
He loved his home in the country.

He snuggled in his kennel where
In a bowl was a steak cooked rare.

He opened one eye and licked the meat.
Was this his meal or just a treat?

He ate a piece and then some more,
But then he heard Jamie roar.

"That's my dinner, my young son.
Where's my pudding, my currant bun?"

Dan crept into his little bed,
Tears falling, his face quite red.

Then Jamie pencilled in his name,
Making sure the bowls were not the same.

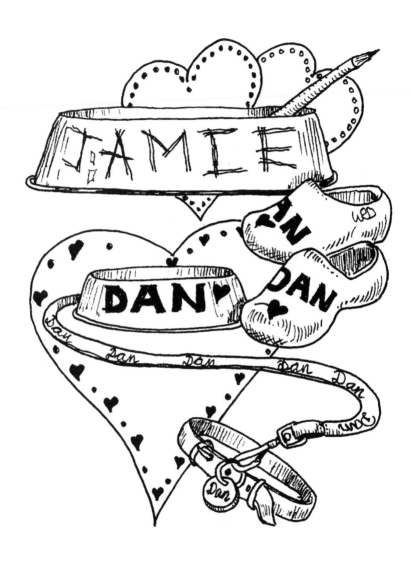

So Dan's name's on his bowl for ever
Together with his clogs and collar.

Draw your own pictures

Draw your own pictures

Colour in yourself

VENTURING OUT

They decided on a little walk
To see their friends and other folk.

Biff and Scott were having fun
And Jealous Joe romped in the sun.

"Can I play?" asked little Dan.
"Yes, dear son, of course you can."

Claire slipped the lead from young Dan's neck;
Dan ran for the river, oh what the heck!

"Dan, you haven't learned to swim,"
Said the postie looking grim.

Jamie and Claire dashed after Dan,
But by the reeds was an old man.

He grabbed Dan's collar nice and neat;
Dan just shivered – he had wet feet.

"Let's get back," said Claire in tears.
The River Test was her worst fear.

Back in the garden, Dan dreamed of mice,
His friends, the river and all things nice.

Draw your own pictures

Draw your own pictures

Colour in yourself